This book may be returned to any Wiltshire
library. To renew this book phone your library
or visit the website: www.wiltshire.gov.uk

*Wiltshire*
COUNTY COUNCIL

CHILDREN, EDUCATION & LIBRARIES

LM6.108.5

D1149079

# Join Buster and his gruesome crew for more piratical adventures!

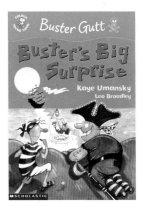

## And why not try some other Colour Young Hippo titles too!

Beetle and Friends

Mermaid Rock

Millie and Bombassa

Sherlock Hound

Creepy Crawlies

Fat Alphie and Charlie the Wimp

Tales from Whispery Wood

Buster Gutt

# Buster Takes a Hostage

## Kaye Umansky
### illustrated by Leo Broadley

■SCHOLASTIC

Scholastic Children's Books,
Commonwealth House, 1-19 New Oxford Street,
London, WC1A 1NU, UK
a division of Scholastic Ltd
London ~ New York ~ Toronto ~ Sydney ~ Auckland
Mexico City ~ New Delhi ~ Hong Kong

First published by Scholastic Ltd, 2004

Text copyright © Kaye Umansky, 2004
Illustrations copyright © Leo Broadley, 2004

ISBN 0 439 97773 8

Printed and bound by Tien Wah Press Pte. Ltd, Singapore

10 9 8 7 6 5 4 3 2 1

The rights of Kaye Umansky and Leo Broadley to be identified as the author
and illustrator of this work respectively have been asserted by them in accordance
with the Copyright, Designs and Patents Act, 1988.

# Chapter One

"Broke," said Buster Gutt, the pirate chief, staring down into his empty treasure chest. "Not a penny, Tiddlefish. Not a bean. Where'd it all go?"

"We shouldn't have gone to Pirate Island," said Timothy Tiddlefish, the cabin boy, who always had a cold. "I said we couldn't a – *achoo!* Afford it."

Pirate Island was a popular holiday resort in the South Seas. It had everything a fun-loving pirate needed – sun, sea, hook and eye-patch stalls, barbecued grub, unlimited rum and a huge punch-up every evening.

Buster and the crew had spent two glorious weeks there.

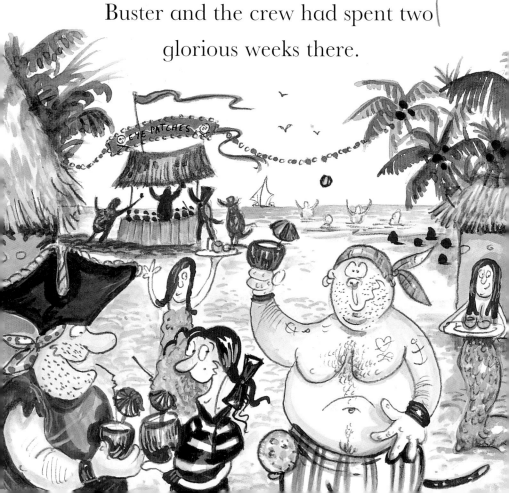

"It were a good 'oliday,
though," sighed Buster,
fingering his black eye.
"Won the punch-up cup,
didn't we?"

They both eyed the big gold cup
which had pride of place in Buster's cabin.

It had been presented to them for winning
the punch-up fourteen nights in a row.
Buster was thrilled with it and swore he
would keep it for ever.

"I suppose we'd better tell the crew," sighed Timothy. "But they're gonna be mad a – a – *achoo!*"

"Why me?" protested Buster. "We all spent it."

"Yes, but the captain's meant to look after the money. You never explained it was *all* gone."

The crew took the news very badly indeed.

"Broke?" cried
Jimmy Maggot,
the cook.

"No goin'
ashore to spend,
spend, spend?" wailed
Crasher Jackson,
the helmsman.

"No tavern
meals?" gasped
Threefingers
Jake, the bosun.

"No toppin' up on the rum?" gulped One-Eyed Ed, the lookout.

"Nope," sighed Buster. "Not till we done some lootin' an' pillagin'."

"An' what am I supposed to cook in the meantime?" demanded Jimmy Maggot. "We're out of everythin' 'cept boiled seaweed."

Everyone made a face. Boiled seaweed tasted awful, like salty knitting.

"All right, so we'll live on Bowzer's octopus scratchin's," said Buster.

Bowzer, the ship's dog, looked worried. He *loved* his octopus scratchings.

"'Tis all very well talkin' about lootin' an' pillagin', Captain," said One-Eyed Ed, "but we ain't seen any ships, 'ave we? Not for days."

This was true. Ever since leaving Pirate Island, the seas had been empty of all but the odd rock.

"Somethin'll turn up," said Buster, trying to sound confident. "Let's take a shifty through the telescope. All 'ands on deck!"

# Chapter Two

Admiral Ainsley Goldglove, the celebrated pirate-catcher, leaned back and sighed contentedly. It had been an excellent supper. Chicken, cherries, cheese and champagne.

The admiral had recently rounded up a record number of pirates, getting a large purse of gold and his picture in the paper for his efforts. Right now his ship, the *HMS Glorious*, was at anchor, and he was enjoying a well-earned rest, away from the cheering crowds.

# ADMIRAL GOLDGLOVE DOES IT AGAIN!

"All finished, sir? Shall I fetch your cash box?" asked Crisply Pimpleby, the first officer, saluting smartly.

The admiral nodded.

"Good idea, Pimpleby." There was nothing he liked better than sitting on deck on a summer evening, counting his money.

"I'll get Plankton to clear away the dishes," said Monty Marshmallow, the chef, and went off to find Private Derek Plankton, who was dusting somewhere.

"Excuse me, Admiral," said Seaman
Scuttle, excitedly approaching the table.
"Ship sighted on the starboard side. Could
be pirates. Shall I wheel
out the cannons?"

"Not now, Scuttle," said the admiral,
testily. "I'm not in the mood for fighting.
All that smoke and noise. I'm letting my
supper go down."

"Excellent decision, sir," said Crisply Pimpleby, staggering up with a huge chest. "It's not as if you're short of cash, is it?"

He threw open the lid with a flourish. It was filled to the brim with gold coins!

"*Sharksbum!* See that?" gasped Buster as they leaned over the rail, gazing at the distant ship. "It's 'im! Goldglove! Sittin' there smirkin' with a load o' posh nosh an' a *chest full o' dosh*!"

"Let's see," said
Timothy Tiddlefish.
He took the
telescope and
put it to his eye.

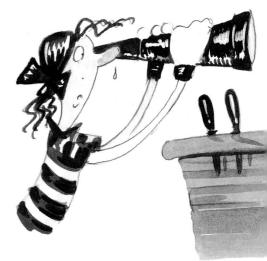

Sure enough, there was the *HMS Glorious*.
And there was the admiral at his table,
stacking gold coins into tall towers.

"It's not fair!" snarled Buster. "'Ow come 'e's got gold an' I ain't? Well, I wants some, *right now*! We'll sail up an' swarm aboard an' grab the loot an—"

"Bad idea," said Timothy.

"Eh? Why?"

"Because they'll see us coming and there'll be a big fight and we'll lose. You don't want the admiral to ca – a – *achoo!* Catch you. Do you?"

"Well, no…" growled Buster.

"Right," said Timothy. "I've got a better idea. Listen…"

# Chapter Three

A big moon hung in the sky. On board the
*HMS Glorious,* everyone had gone to bed,
apart from Private Derek Plankton, who
was still clearing up. He had washed the
dishes and swept up the crumbs. He was
now hard at work polishing the table.

He was so busy, he didn't hear the creak of approaching oars. He only became aware that something was afoot when a blanket came down over his head and he found himself being manhandled over the side and down into a rowing boat.

When the blanket was finally removed, he found himself standing on the deck of *The Bad Joke*, surrounded by Buster's motley crew.

"Hello, Derek," said Timothy Tiddlefish. "We've taken you hostage. Sorry."

"Oh," said Private Derek Plankton. He nibbled his duster. "Will it hurt?"

"Course not," said Buster, a bit put out. "What d'you take us for?"

"Um – pirates?" guessed Private Derek Plankton. He reached down and gave Bowzer a little pat. Bowzer licked his hand.

"Well, yeah," agreed Buster. "Yeah, we're *pirates*. But we ain't got nothin' against you. 'Tis Goldglove we don't like. We're 'oldin' you ransom till 'e coughs up a hundred gold coins."

"We'll send you ba – a – *achoo!* – back safe and sound, as soon as it a – *achoo!* – arrives," promised Timothy.

"All right," said Private Derek Plankton, with a shrug. "What'll I do till then?"

"Whatever you like, long as you don't try to escape," said Buster. "Bowzer! Guard the prisoner."

Bowzer wagged his tail. He loved Private Derek Plankton.

It wasn't until the following morning that Admiral Ainsley Goldglove discovered Private Derek Plankton gone and a ransom note pinned to the mast with a dagger. It read:

HA HA
I GOT PLANKTON
GIV US 100
GOLD KOINS
BUSTER GUTT

"See this?" raged
the admiral.
"What a cheek!"

"Dear me," said
Crisply Pimpleby.
"This is a bad
business. Will
you pay up, sir?"

"What, and let Gutt get one over on me?
Certainly not! Man the cannons! We'll sink
his ship."

"But what about Plankton? He'll sink with it," said Crisply Pimpleby, uneasily.

"So?"

"But it's not done, sir, sinking one of your own men. What if the papers find out?"

"Hmm." The admiral looked thoughtful. "All right, forget the cannon. But I'm not paying a penny. I shall play a waiting game. And in the meantime, *you* can do the cleaning."

#  Chapter Four

Back on board *The Bad Joke*, Buster had just
got a bad surprise. "Oh no!" he groaned.
"Look what 'e's done to my ship!"

*The Bad Joke* was unrecognizable. It
gleamed. It shone. It had been dusted,
swept, scrubbed and buffed. The holes in
the sails had been neatly mended. Even
Bowzer had been given a bath!

Right now, Private Derek Plankton was high up the rigging, rehanging the Jolly Roger which had been washed, ironed and dyed pink.

"He must have been a – *achoo!* – at it all night," gasped Timothy.

"You should see my galley!" wailed Jimmy Maggot. "He's scraped the burnt bits off the pots! I liked them burnt bits. The burnt bits is where you get all the flavour."

"He put a vase o' flowers in my cabin," growled Crasher Jackson. "*Flowers!* Where'd he get flowers in the middle of the ocean?"

"I keep falling over, where he's oiled the deck," complained One-Eyed Ed, rubbing his shin. "He's dangerous, he is."

"Any news about the ransom?" Buster asked Timothy Tiddlefish, hopefully.

"No," said Timothy, glumly.

"Perhaps we're askin' too much," said Buster. "Perhaps we should take a bit less."

Everyone agreed that perhaps a hundred gold coins *was* a bit much.

Some time later, on board the *HMS Glorious,*
Crisply Pimpleby trailed up and presented
the admiral with a soggy piece of paper.

"What's this?" snapped the admiral.

"Another message from Gutt, sir.
Arrived in a bottle."

Crisply Pimpleby stifled a yawn. Cleaning was *hard*. His back hurt. He had accidentally squirted polish in his eye. The frilly apron didn't suit him.

However hard he tried, he simply couldn't keep up with the mess. He hoped Private Derek Plankton would be released soon.

The admiral snatched the note. It read:

AWL RITE
50

Over on *The Bad Joke*, Private Derek Plankton was polishing cannonballs and arranging them in a tidy pile.

"I'm gonna stop 'im," announced Buster. "I can't stand watchin', it's drivin' me mad."

"You said he could – *achoo!* – do whatever he liked," Timothy reminded him.

"Well, I've changed me mind. Either 'e stops cleanin' or 'e goes overboard."

"Then we won't have a hostage," Timothy pointed out.

"So? Ain't no sign o' the ransom."

"Perhaps fifty's pushin' it a bit," said Threefingers Jake. "Maybe we should go for thirty?"

"Try for twenty," moaned Crasher Jackson. "Let's get rid of 'im."

"Ten," pleaded One-Eyed Ed. "Just to be on the safe side."

"Ten it is, then," sighed
Buster, and he stomped
off to his cabin to write
yet another
ransom
note.

☠ ☠ ☠

"Another one's arrived sir," yawned Crisply
Pimpleby. "Dropped by a seagull this
time." Tiredly, he held out the note, which
read:

"You see?" chortled the admiral. "He's
cracking!"

"Can't we pay up, sir?" pleaded Crisply Pimpleby. He had just finished scrubbing the deck, only to find a flock of seagulls had undone all his good work.

"No chance," said the admiral. "We stick to our guns. Or in your case, the mop. Come along, man, get cleaning! That deck's a disgrace!"

A short time later, another note arrived, by arrow this time.

"Down to five, I see," said the admiral, crumpling it up and throwing it into the sea.

He did the same to the next four.

That night, when darkness fell, a small rowing boat nudged against the stern of the *HMS Glorious*. In it, was Private Derek Plankton. Pinned on his hat was a final message. It read:

The next morning everyone was pleased to find Private Derek Plankton back on board ship.

"Well done, Plankton," said the admiral. "You kept your head and saved me money. I feel a small reward is in order. What would you like?"

Private Derek Plankton thought about it. "Well, I could do with a new duster."

Back on board *The Bad Joke*, Buster and the boys sat gloomily on deck, eating boiled seaweed. The ship was spick and span and smelled of lemons.

"I 'ates it," grumbled Buster. "Don't feel like 'ome any more."

"Cheer up, Captain," said Timothy, consolingly. "We'll soon mess it up again."

"All that, and we're still broke," said Buster.

"Ah well. You win some, you – *achoo!* – lose some. What do we do now?"

Buster gave a little sigh. His eyes flickered around the cabin and landed on his favourite thing. "The way I see it," he said, "there's only one thing we *can* do."

So this is what they did. They sailed back to Pirate Island ...

... sold the punch-up cup to a rival crew ...

... spent the proceeds on another rip-roaring holiday ...

... and ended up
broke again!